RETIREMENT

Dedicated to those who believe that youth is a gift of nature, but age is a work of art.

NAME

FROM

DATE

Copyright © 1989, Great Quotations, Inc.

All rights reserved. No part of this publication may be reproduced, stored in a retrieval system, or transmitted in any form or by any means, electronic, mechanical, photocopying, recording or otherwise without the prior consent of Great Quotations, Inc.

ISBN: 0-931089-82-4

A Special Message:

*Retirement —
when every day
is Saturday.*

The more sand that has escaped from the hourglass of our life, the clearer we should see through it.

Life is a gift, to live is an opportunity, to give is an obligation, and to grow old is a privilege.

Candy Hughes

Age is a matter of mind; if you don't mind, it doesn't matter.

Retirement: the period when you stop quoting the proverb that time is money.

Youth is a gift of nature, but age is a work of art.

Judy Barry

Anyone who keeps the ability to see beauty never grows old.

Franz Kafka

Growing older we learn miracles are great, but they are so darn unpredictable.

The worst thing about retirement is to have to drink coffee on your own time.

Retire — not from something, but to something.

Age does not depend upon years, but upon temperament and health. Some men are born old, and some never grow so.

Tryon Edwards

*Retirement
is the time of life
when you stop
lying about your
age and start lying
about the house.*

Age ... is a matter of feeling, not of years.

George William Curtis

Growing older means realizing that our life is what our thoughts make of it.

We do not stop playing because we are old; we grow old because we stop playing.

I'm old enough to know the rules and smart enough to break them.

Youth is wasted on the young.

As we grow older, we learn that the wisest man is usually he who thinks himself the least so.

You are young at any age if you are planning for tomorrow.

Lulline T. Hodges

We neither get better nor worse as we get older, but more like ourselves.

                        Sr. Robert Anthony

The challenge to retirement is to figure out how to spend time without spending money.

The aging process is a lot like grapes — some turn to vinegar but the best turn to wine.

You're in the prime of your life — it just takes a little longer to get primed.

A wife's definition of retirement: "Twice as much husband, and half as much income."

The older we get, the more we realize — after all is said and done, more is said than done.

Wrinkles are only the bypaths of many smiles.

There's many a good tune played on an old fiddle.

*Peace is
when time
doesn't matter
as it passes by.*

Maria Schell

Years teach us that knowledge becomes wisdom only after it has been put to practical use.

Accept the changes age brings and stay alive inside.

Youth is the time for the adventure of the body, but age, triumphs of the mind.

Logan Pearsall Smith

Retirement is the beginning of a new career. We find ourselves doing what we really wanted to do — but could not for most of our lives.

To be fifty years young is sometimes more cheerful and hopeful than to be twenty years old.

The secret of a long life is double careers. One to about age 60, then another for the next 30 years.

Regardless of their age, most folks are not as old as they hope to be.

*The secret . . .
Find an age and
stick to it.*

Sixty and sensational. Seventy and celebrating.

When a man retires and time is no longer a matter of urgent importance, his colleagues generally present him with a clock.

Smart enough to know better, old enough not to care.

Youth is the time of getting, middle age of improving, and old age of spending.

In this life the old believe everything, the middle-aged suspect everything, and the young know everything.

At your age you don't have to act responsible.

Retirement is wonderful if you have two essentials: much to live on and much to live for.

After retirement golfers only play golf on days ending with "y."

Old enough to know your limit, young enough to exceed it.

The key to retirement is to have enough money to live on, but not enough to worry about.

Hardening of the heart ages people more quickly than hardening of the arteries.

*As we age
we learn
riches are mental,
not material.*

Some hearts, like evening primroses, open more beautifully in the shadows of life.

Sarah Wells

You have to climb the mountain to appreciate the beauty of the view.

So long as the heart receives messages of beauty, hope, cheer, and courage, you will be young.

If wrinkles must be written upon our brows, let them not be written upon the heart. The spirit should never grow old.

James A. Garfield

Growing old wisely means making more opportunities than we find.

Only when your heart is covered with the snows of pessimism and ice of cynicism do you grow old.

Years wrinkle the skin, but to give up enthusiasm wrinkles the soul.

Retirement is when a man who figured he'd go fishing seven times a week finds himself washing the dishes three times a day.

In spite of the cost of living, it's still popular.

The longer we live, the more we learn it is not who has the most — it is who makes the most of what he has.

A man is not old as long as he is seeking something.

Jean Rostand

You are as young as your self-confidence, as old as your despair.

We live in deeds, not years, in thoughts, not breaths, in feelings, not in figures on the dial.

G. Baily

As we grow older and wiser, we talk less and say more.

*We grow
old as soon as
we cease to love
and trust.*

Madame de Choiseul

Growing gracefully slower of step is only walking nearer to God.

*Take care
that old age
does not wrinkle
your spirit.*

Don't laugh at old age — some folks never make it.

The tide of life is sometimes very rough, but each storm ridden through makes us a better captain of our souls.

No one grows old by merely living a number of years. People grow old only by deserting their ideas.

Age stiffens the joints but softens the heart.

No one grows old by living — only by losing interest in living.

It's up to us whether age brings wisdom or age comes alone.

A man is not old until regrets take the place of dreams.

Young at heart, slightly older in other places.

You can't help getting older, but you don't have to get old.

Retirement can be a catastrophe or a commencement, a rocking chair or a launching pad.

The tomorrow you worried about is better than the yesterday.

Other Great Quotations Books:

- The Book of Proverbs
- Aged to Perfection
- Retirement
- Love on Your Wedding Day
- Thinking of You
- The Unofficial Executive Survival Guide
- Inspirations
- Sports Poop
- Over the Hill
- Golf Humor
- Happy Birthday to the Golfer
- Stress
- Cat Tales
- The Unofficial Christmas Survival Guide
- The Unofficial Survival Guide To Parenthood
- A Smile Increases Your Face Value
- Keys to Happiness
- Things You'll Learn...
- Teachers Inspirations
- Boyfriends Live Longer than...
- Worms of Wisdom
- Our Life Together
- Thoughts from the Heart
- An Apple a Day
- The Joy of Family
- What to Tell Your Children
- Proverbs Vol. II
- A Friend is a Present
- Books are Better in Bed than Men

GREAT QUOTATIONS, INC.
1967 Quincy Ct. • Glendale Heights, IL 60139

TOLL FREE: 800-354-4889 (outside Illinois)
(708) 582-2800
PRINTED IN HONG KONG